RHYME CRAFT

Essex Voices

Edited By Donna Samworth

First published in Great Britain in 2018 by:

YoungWriters

Young Writers
Remus House
Coltsfoot Drive
Peterborough
PE2 9BF
Telephone: 01733 890066
Website: www.youngwriters.co.uk

All Rights Reserved
Book Design by Ashley Janson
© Copyright Contributors 2017
SB ISBN 978-1-78896-163-9
Printed and bound in the UK by BookPrintingUK
Website: www.bookprintinguk.com
YB0348A

FOREWORD

Welcome, Reader, to *Rhymecraft - Essex Voices*.

Among these pages you will find a whole host of poetic gems, built from the ground up by some wonderful young minds. Included are a variety of poetic styles, from amazing acrostics to creative cinquains, from dazzling diamantes to fascinating free verse.

Here at Young Writers our objective has always been to help children discover the joys of poetry and creative writing. Few things are more encouraging for the aspiring writer than seeing their own work in print. We are proud that our anthologies are able to give young authors this unique sense of confidence and pride in their abilities as well as letting their poetry reach new audiences.

The editing process was a tough but rewarding one that allowed us to gain an insight into the blooming creativity of today's primary school pupils. I hope you find as much enjoyment and inspiration in the following poetry as I have, so much so that you pick up a pen and get writing!

Donna Samworth

CONTENTS

Independent Entries

Madeleine Grace Scott (9)	1
Kyla Marie Angeles Datu (8)	2
Afnan Ahmed (10)	4
Advait Devdutt (7)	5
Jake Smith	6

Downham CE (VC) Primary School, Ramsden Heath

Olivia Josephine Cross (8)	7
Ava Bruty (8)	8
Scarlett Hicks (6)	9
Emily Gutteridge (8)	10

East Tilbury Primary School, East Tilbury

Kimberley Isla McCann (8)	11
Isabelle Oakley (10)	12
Jimmie Holbird (9)	13
Holly Cuzner (10)	14
Alfie Dove-Webb (8)	15
Holly Farr (10)	16
Jude William George Fraser-Ramsey (10)	17
Oliver Emerson (8)	18
Eliana Sesifredo (9)	19
Roxanne (10) & Aleyna Sesifrado	20
Emma Raynham (8)	21

Gearies Primary School, Gants Hill

Ibrahim Kashif (11)	22
Aadi Nair (10)	24
Safwaan Shareef (9)	26
Hakan Coskun (7)	28
Hannah Mannan (9)	30
Siyonaa Banerjee (10)	31
Rafay Idrees (10)	32
Khadijah Siddiqah (10)	33
Anna-Maria Dimitrova (9)	34
Sharwin Krishna (9)	35
Areesha Haque (10)	36
Miha Aleksander Folkson (10)	37
Safwan Hasan (9)	38
Nabiha Farbin (11)	39
Harish Ganesalingam (10)	40
Sofia Woodruffe (9)	41
Rhiyaa Sasitharan (9)	42
Birrah Rana (8)	43
Nabiha Sajid (10)	44
Sara Howlader (9)	45
Punyatoa Roy (9)	46
Vinuki Vidara Buddhadasa (11)	47
Manishaa Senthilkumaran (9)	48
Rayaan Ahmed (9)	49
Avneet Kaur Degun (10)	50
Forhad Al Mahfuz (10)	51
Faiza Shahid (9)	52
Sriansh Panda (7)	53
Bishal Roy (11)	54
Parija Miral Popat (8)	55
Aksharra Vidhyaprakash	56
Armaan Gorthy (8)	57
Sufyan Akbar Rashid (10)	58
Rok Gustav Folkson (7)	59
Adyan Alam (7)	60

Gidea Park Primary School, Gidea Park

Sydney Maffey (10), Macie Lily Crosby & Sam	61
Teddy Short (9)	62
Alexandra Hopkins (10)	64

Great Totham Primary School, Great Totham

Eliza Dundas (7)	66
Toby Woodman (7)	68
Summer Nicole Jarvis (7)	69
Lauren Ferguson (7)	70
Emily Seabright (7)	71
Gracie-Lou Redgrove (7)	72
Emma Hull (7)	73
Jake Sutton Moss (7)	74
Haydn Court (7)	75
Molly Anna Surgett (7)	76
Rose Poppy Surgett (7)	77
Autumn-Rose Heeley (7)	78
Lucy White (7)	79

Harwich Community Primary School & Nursery, Harwich

Summer Lambert (11)	80
Gracie White (10)	81
Drew Beezley (10)	82
Chelsea Kelly (9)	83
Maxim Bowgen (10)	84
Gracie Mae Kadar (9)	85
Evangeline J Shephard (10)	86
Caitlin Ruby Isabel Barham (10)	87
Sophie Louise Fuller (9)	88
Henry Alexander Michael Lammas (9)	89
Eliza Betty Hyams-Morgan (10)	90
Lily Knight (10)	91
Kaceyleigh Garlick (10)	92
Penny Stacey (8)	93

Highfields Primary School, Lawford

Olivia Stone (11)	94
Isabelle Marshall (9)	95
Molly Quinn Finch (9)	96
Joshua James Gerrard Bird (9)	97
Nicolas Kumai-Girard (9)	98

Parsloes Primary School, Dagenham

Rhemson Nzolameso (9)	99
Zbigniew Chertlur (8)	100

Priory Primary School, Bicknacre

Joseph Archer (7)	101
Esther Stickley (8)	102
Isabella Crome (8)	103
Eleanor Border (8)	104
Alana Lloyd (8)	105
Darcy Sofia Rogers (7)	106
Ruby-Tallulah Smith (8)	107
Ellie-Rae Ward (7)	108
Jude Platt (7)	109
Marina Burchea (7)	110
Alfie Webb (7)	111
Jamie Russell (7)	112
Callum Lowe (7)	113
Drew Almond (7)	114
Molly Rosam (8)	115
Beth Miller (7)	116
Jessica Meadow Healey (7)	117
Thomas Power (8)	118
Luca Chatten (8)	119
Lily Morrish (7)	120

St Anne Line Catholic Junior School, Wickhay

Emma Beardwell (10)	121
Joel Jibu (10)	122
Tyra Nyakunengwa (10)	123
Steve Nevin (10)	124

Gabriel Kijanczuk (9)   125
Tonna Obidi (10)   126

St Joseph's Catholic Primary School, Dagenham

Michelle Mpamugo (10)   127
Favour Omoradion (10)   128
Stephaine Fope Akinnawonu (10)   130
Emile Zubkus (8)   131
Lexi Cooper (8)   132
Tomiwa Alaitan (9)   133
Amelia Clare Lloyd (7)   134

Trinity School, Kelvedon Hatch

Zack Cristescu (10)   135
Joy Mungai-Kimani (10)   136

THE POEMS

The Magic Ride

Neigh, neigh, what is that?
A second ago I was feeding my cat!
Am I really seeing this?
Is this really true?
Am I really seeing a unicorn stuck in pink goo?

I'd better go save this unicorn,
It was late so I had a quick yawn,
What a cool place with snow on the ground,
I can see the galaxy all around.

I love this galaxy, I only had a little tear
This is mysterious, how am I here?
Slowly, I walked up to the cutest unicorn in the world,
She had sparkly white curls.

'Thank you, lovely unicorn,' I said
And all of a sudden, I was back in bed.

Madeleine Grace Scott (9)

Cats And Dogs

Let's look at these pet animals,
Their pleasant barks or miaowing calls,
I find some different cons or pros
That'll make your thoughts of them high or low.

I found out that cats are nice,
They get rid of unwanted mice,
But they might ruin your favourite slippers,
And usually escape to your happy neighbours.

Large pups are great for the police,
Bringing guidance, safety and lots of peace,
Though they dig holes in your backyard,
Which, for me, is pretty hard.

Cats and dogs always fight,
Honestly, they give me a fright,
But none of us can choose between them,
Their pros and cons are fairly even.

Now we have learned our lessons,
We all have different opinions,

Cats and dogs are equally great,
As long as they don't scream at your gate!

Kyla Marie Angeles Datu (8)

Fire

Red-hot fire spreads,
Enveloping its victim in dread
The temperature you wish was there,
Now seems as though it's dead.

The winter looks so far away,
It's all you want for a hot summer's day,
The grasp of fire
Is impossible to bear,
It will lure you
To stand in its way.

It may wreck the whole land,
But the appearance is truly grand,
The mess it leaves is not too great,
Buildings can't afford to stand.

Afnan Ahmed (10)

My Wish For A Big Friend

I wish I had a friend
big like a giant.
He would be very funny
and cute like a bunny.
I would call him Bubbles
and give him cuddles.
He would carry me to school
and that would be cool.
Together we will be the best
better than the rest.

Advait Devdutt (7)

Macbeth Diary

Ever since
I think she is a witch
I can't go on
She is just killing me
If I don't do it
My life is gone
I feel
She is looking at me
All she wants is blood
But I don't
She is just a killer.

Jake Smith

Space

S o far somewhere I can see stars clashing to make a galaxy.
P laces and planets crashing together, that's not what I want to see.
A liens of all shapes and sizes, big, small, short and tall.
C arry on looking, just wait and see...
E normous planets crushing, crumbling.

Olivia Josephine Cross (8)
Downham CE (VC) Primary School, Ramsden Heath

Cute And Cuddly

Animals are cuddly and snuggly,
But some are fierce and ugly,
Up in the trees,
Monkeys, gorillas, orangutans,
You're one too!

Animals are slimy and creepy,
But some can be mean and sneaky,
Down, down, deep,
Sharks, dolphins, manta rays.
Are you good at swimming?

Ava Bruty (8)
Downham CE (VC) Primary School, Ramsden Heath

Make It Better

U nhappy people running around
N o such thing!
I can save the day with my unicorn horn
C onquer the world
O bviously yes!
R oaring through the sky
N aughty old goblins
S top them now!

Scarlett Hicks (6)
Downham CE (VC) Primary School, Ramsden Heath

Space

S pace is a lovely place
P lanets are very nice, they look fascinating
A liens look very weird flying in their ships!
C olours and shapes, like you have never seen before
E xciting adventures in space!

Emily Gutteridge (8)
Downham CE (VC) Primary School, Ramsden Heath

Build Your World

B uild your world
U se those blocks
I cy diamonds
L ava rocks
D ig and dig and dig some more

Y ield your weapons
O wn the war
U nderground you can play
R edstone, dirt and even clay

W ondrous oceans, fields of grass
O pen caves and homes of glass
R eality and fantasy blur together
L ive in this world, no matter the weather
D ig and dig and dig some more, don't stop until you reach the core.

Kimberley Isla McCann (8)
East Tilbury Primary School, East Tilbury

Fun! Fun! Fun!

Try and make a great big house
Minecraft is a game for fun
Watch out! There are mobs behind you
Now you need to run, run, run!
This will be a bad time to brew
When you have time, brew swiftness potions
These make you faster than you could dream
Beacons make a great big beam

Minecraft is a fun game to play
Maybe they'll add a massive ray
This is a game to play with friends
Rather than play alone
Everyone should play
Try it one day.

Isabelle Oakley (10)
East Tilbury Primary School, East Tilbury

My Minecraft Life

Mining and building, that's what I do for fun
Shape it, form it, right under the sun
My name is Steve and I mine in my time
My favourite stone would be the stone of the lime
I have a girlfriend called Alice and her hair is curled
She mines and lives with me in my Minecraft world
I mine through the day,
From January to May
As the sun sets, I lock up my pig,
Throw on my jacket for my night and head out
to dig.

Jimmie Holbird (9)
East Tilbury Primary School, East Tilbury

The Wonderful World Of Minecraft

M ountains towering tall
I gloos with an icy block wall
N asty creatures lurking
E ndless possibilities await
C reate a world of blocky buildings up so tall
R ivers and waterfalls rushing down
A mazing discoveries have been found
F arm animals lying around
T he world of endless creation.

Holly Cuzner (10)
East Tilbury Primary School, East Tilbury

Crafty Poem

My house is built of cobblestones
I slayed a skeleton, who dropped a bone
I found a dragon egg nearby
And as I looked up in the sky
I saw a three-headed ghast
Flying towards me, super fast
I pulled out my sword and hit it twice
Then I saw some endermites
One swing and they were gone
The Minecraft hacker is the song!

Alfie Dove-Webb (8)
East Tilbury Primary School, East Tilbury

My Maisie!

My Maisie is my pony
Sometimes my Maisie can be a bit lazy
She is still my pony
Sometimes my Maisie can be a little bit crazy
She is still my pony
My Maisie is as pretty as a daisy
She is still my pony
With my Maisie pony, I will never be lonely
She is my pony
I love my Maisie pony.

Holly Farr (10)
East Tilbury Primary School, East Tilbury

Minecraft, Most Annoying Mobs

Endermen, Endermen
stay out of their sight
because they have a very tall height!

Pigs, pigs
as far as I can see
filled with pork chops
ready for me to eat.

Squids, squids
annoying swimming creatures
I always wondered
what is the point of squid?

Jude William George Fraser-Ramsey (10)
East Tilbury Primary School, East Tilbury

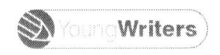

Mobs Mayhem

M obs are unkind
O bjects getting destroyed
B oxing, they are good
S lithering snakes

M ad trust
A ctive horror movie
Y ou'll be scared
H elp!
E xciting scariness
M ayhem alert!

Oliver Emerson (8)
East Tilbury Primary School, East Tilbury

Cubes

Cubes, cubes everywhere
everywhere, but not my hair.
On my body, on my feet
on my toes, on my knees.
My house is made of cubes, so is my door
I've got cubes on my floor.
We all just want some more.
We all love cubes.
Yes! More cubes.

Eliana Sesifredo (9)
East Tilbury Primary School, East Tilbury

The Magical Land Of Cubes

Dogs, dogs, dogs are just cubes,
Cats, birds were cubes too,
Cubes on my roof,
Cubes on my floor,
We just can't take it anymore.
Bows, hats, phones and beds,
Pillows that we use on our heads,
Too many cubes,
No more, no more!

Roxanne (10) & Aleyna Sesifrado
East Tilbury Primary School, East Tilbury

The Mine

M agnificent mine
I nside is as dark as an abandoned house
N asty creatures all over the place
E xcellent creatures and things you can find.

Emma Raynham (8)
East Tilbury Primary School, East Tilbury

The Ambitious Miner

Once there lived this man
Who loved to mine
Although he dug a lot
His findings were never actually fine.

Occasionally he found old, battered boots
Along with bits of fake gold
He thought it was really real
As that was what he was told.

One time he dug so much
He wanted to rest so badly
But was forced to go on
So he started whispering to himself sadly.

One dark, dull, depressing day
He thought about giving up
Then was like, 'No way!'
And started to drink from his favourite cup.

The next day, he was full of hope
Knowing this might be his lucky day

So he packed his compass, torch and rope
And started to set away.

It was as dark as a never-ending abyss
Full of blood-curdling scares
Then he thought he saw something
Realising it was just stunning pears.

His heart began pounding
As the light closed on him
The beautiful gold was so astounding
He just stood there, eyes going dim.

He took all of it
Leaving nothing
Then he nearly fell into a pit
Which was something?

Ibrahim Kashif (11)
Gearies Primary School, Gants Hill

My Nightmares

Every day I would have a nightmare,
It can be in a desert or outer space,
But this time it was in a castle.

I stalked around, looking for an exit,
Away from my horrendous nightmare,
I found a peculiar-looking bridge,
Suddenly, as I was walking across the bridge,
A red, ferocious dragon burnt the bridge with
A powerful ray of fire.

I ran around the castle,
Running away from the giant, ferocious dragon,
Passageways and secret tunnels confused the dragon,
I kept running and running away from the dragon
As I was running, I thought of an answer
To all these nightmares... which hid.

All my nightmares had a shining light in it,
As I was one door away from the light,
The dragon suddenly became frantic,

It used Power Dive and destroyed the roof,
Which blocked the door,
But I could just crawl under the clutter,
And stop it for good.

I found myself in my bed thinking,
I should stop watching all these,
Scary movies.

Aadi Nair (10)
Gearies Primary School, Gants Hill

Operation Cake!

I glance from one to another, to see my mother
We went to the shop, then the bus stop and went back home
A satisfying smell triggered my nose
What was it? Who knows?
Then I found out that it was a cake
That my mum had baked
I was about to take a slice
But my mum said it was not nice!
She was preparing it for guests
The cake was the best
Now for Operation Cake!
Mum usually wakes up, seven in the morning
And Dad is always snoring
So I should wake up at five
Only to save my life
Going deep into sleep
Wake up!
Five-thirty!
Continue to plan...
Down the stairs, into the kitchen

Now don't act like a chicken
Where is the plate?
It's going to be too late!
Take the layer and go!

Safwaan Shareef (9)
Gearies Primary School, Gants Hill

The Black And White Cat

Hello, black and white cat,
I see you in my garden!
Searching for something
and making a mess,
without any pardon!
But it's OK,
I can see you're distressed,
perhaps you're looking for food
or somewhere to rest!
The sky is getting dark,
do you want to come inside?
It's warm in here,
and I'll feed you lots of chicken pies!
Please don't run away black and white cat,
there's no need to be scared!
I'm not here to hurt you
or to give you a scare.
I know it might take a lot of time
for us to be friends
but I'll do whatever it takes
I must gain your trust.

Goodbye black and white cat,
I hope I'll see you again!

Hakan Coskun (7)
Gearies Primary School, Gants Hill

The Black Cat

In a mysterious alleyway, a shadow appears,
it has yellow eyes and pointy ears.
He glides from bin to bin,
and gives his tail a spin.

His fur is as black as the dead of night,
this unusual moggy loathes the light.
His miniature paws are covered in mud,
they are soft and padded and don't make a thud.

He consumes fish and morsels of food,
this puts him in a cheerful mood.
Whatever you do, don't give him jelly,
otherwise he will have an upset belly.

Cats are smart and wonderful creatures,
they have many interesting features.
Instead of a girl I would like to be a cat,
if you are lucky, you may see me on your mat!

Hannah Mannan (9)
Gearies Primary School, Gants Hill

Shadows

Dark shadows wander in the night,
Making people leap with fright,
On the oily-black pavements, they scamper around,
Wait! Did you hear a sound?
No lights, no sign, nothing but the pitch-black sky,
Awake in bed, I lie,
My face sheet-white,
My lips pulled tight,
I watch the sinister figments on my wall,
Some short and some tall,
My eyes turn blood-red with fear,
I'm too frightened to cry or drop a tear,
I feel as if something will grab me,
Suddenly, my hands start shaking by what I see,
An immense figure with one razor-sharp claw,
I think it likes eating things that are raw,
Just as it comes near,
The figure disappears, I am glad morning is here.

Siyonaa Banerjee (10)
Gearies Primary School, Gants Hill

Minecraft Friends

M ining in the game
I want it to be the same
N ever will I get it
E veryone took a hit
C rafting my diamond sword
R evealing my diamond horde
A fter all these years
F reeing none of my tears
T rapped inside of me

F orgotten not, is my friends' memories, you see
R aw was the giant war
I will never forget those sad days
E specially when I saw my friends' items inside of trays
N oise of my friends ring inside my head
D on't make me think they're really dead
S adness is the only thing I will ever be.

Rafay Idrees (10)
Gearies Primary School, Gants Hill

Lost Or Found?

Being lost is like your heart being ripped out
Feeling like you're the only person
Everything is pitch-black
Looking around, searching for help.

Being lost is like when you've been grabbed
Feeling as if someone's creeping up on you
Everything is pitch-black
Where am I? What should I do?

Being found is the most happiest moment!
Feeling like you're going to burst into tears
Everything is yellow and blue
The sun is shining.

Being found is like finding a key to a maze
Feeling like the whole world knows
Everything is watching, even the clouds
The trees are clapping in joy!

Khadijah Siddiqah (10)
Gearies Primary School, Gants Hill

Flowers

So many flowers you can see
I have got that feeling inside me
When I see one I jump
When I look at the sky up
When I have a shower
I always think of flowers
There are flowers that are red
I think of them when I am on my bed
There are flowers that are pink
When I see one, I always think
There are flowers that are green
That are always seen
There are flowers that are white
Sometimes in the parks they are always in sight
There are flowers that are blue
When I see one I always move
Flowers, they can be nearly all of the colours
Don't you think?

Anna-Maria Dimitrova (9)
Gearies Primary School, Gants Hill

Survival Craft

S limy little creatures slithered along
U seful items, used to defend
R are, magical mobs wandered
V ertical straight up in the mountains
I nside my humble abode
V anishing beasts also there
A dvanced weaponry in hand
L uscious land all to myself

C reepy-crawlies hanging on me
R aw foods cooked and devoured
A fter dawn, I can come out
F abulous clothes are made for me
T he life, my life was there.

Sharwin Krishna (9)
Gearies Primary School, Gants Hill

Grenfell Tower

Lots of precious moments,
never came to back to us.
The cruel blaze of fire,
burnt our heart.
Dedicated group of fighters,
save people to start.
The beloved were screaming,
for the sake of life.
The man was searching,
'Where is my wife?'
The baby was crawling,
his brother's bike.
His empty eyes were searching,
what he saw he did not like.
You're not alone, never think,
I am with you,
the whole picture comes,
when my eyes blink.

Areesha Haque (10)
Gearies Primary School, Gants Hill

Boring Life

I went to the kitchen to cook
My dad didn't even let me look
I went to the living room and went to play the piano
But my brother said, 'You can't play unless you give me your Kinder Bueno.'
I went to the bedroom to read a book
But my mum said, 'I thought you were going to cook?'
I went to the garden and babi said, 'I beg your pardon?
What are you doing in my vegetable garden?'
In the end I went to school
My teacher said, 'That's really cool!'

Miha Aleksander Folkson (10)
Gearies Primary School, Gants Hill

Wizard Dream

W izarding is fun but dangerous
I love it, I can do whatever I want
Z ooming on broomsticks like lightning
A subject is always fun
R acing on dragons always have to be done
D aring wizards love a duel

D reading to tell
R eminding myself not to fall in the well
E ating chocolates, I fell
A reckless wizard I am
M y mum shouts in my ear, 'Quick! Get ready, it's time for school!'

Safwan Hasan (9)
Gearies Primary School, Gants Hill

Things

I like books,
I like books about crooks,
I like hens,
I also like pens,
I like fashion,
It's one of my passions,
I like to eat,
And I don't like to drop the beat,
What do you like?
I want a new bike,
I like being lost,
But it has a cost,
I don't like being alone,
But I don't want a clone,
There are many things that I like,
Many I dislike,
But there are many more things to discover,
What do you take interest in?

Nabiha Farbin (11)
Gearies Primary School, Gants Hill

In My Bedtime Dream

In my bedtime dream,
I woke up near a stream,
The ground was full of fog,
Out came thousands of dogs.

In my bedtime dream,
I woke up near a stream,
A zombie poured over some brains,
And my T-shirt got a stain.

In my bedtime dream,
I woke up near a stream,
An elephant got me a leaf,
Inside was very cheap.

In my bedtime dream,
I woke up near a stream,
I saw a clown,
He came to town.

Harish Ganesalingam (10)
Gearies Primary School, Gants Hill

Colours!

What is white? A cloud is white, all fluffy and bright!
What is yellow? A daffodil is yellow, standing in the meadow!
What is blue? The sea is blue, it makes quite a view!
What is green? An apple is green, that falls from the trees!
What is gold? Money is gold, that shines when it moves.
What is brown? My hair is brown, that sticks out as I frown.
What is red? A bow is red, that stands out on my head.
What is orange? Just an orange! Why, an orange!

Sofia Woodruffe (9)
Gearies Primary School, Gants Hill

The Day I Went To School!

The day I went to school, it was hot, bright and sunny,
The day I went to school, Dad told a joke which was funny,
The day I went to school, children went to their classes,
The day I went to school, the teacher looked through her glasses,
The day I went to school, we looked upon the board,
The day I went to school, the boys played with some cord,
The day I went to school, I learnt something new,
The day I went to school, I bumped into you!

Rhiyaa Sasitharan (9)
Gearies Primary School, Gants Hill

Octocure

Oliver the octopus was feeling rather ill
He went to see the doctopus, who sent him for a pill
He said, 'That's chickpoctapus, your tentacles are spotty.'
Poor Olly got a shocktopus, he felt a little grotty
He bought four pairs of socktopus, to hide his spotty legs
He fed himself on choctopus and jellyfish eggs
In just a week the octopus felt better than before
The spots were gone, the doctopus found the perfect cure!

Birrah Rana (8)
Gearies Primary School, Gants Hill

Unicorn

Enchantingly pure
My eyes aren't really sure
Whether this is a dream
Or just a little scheme
My eyes are fixed
Like they've been bewitched
Have I been cursed?
Oh, how I do need a nurse!

Enchantingly pure
I'm adjusted to the moor
It gives a little whine
While it twitches its eye
My friends tell me not to believe in such things
But what do I do now I know it exists?

Nabiha Sajid (10)
Gearies Primary School, Gants Hill

What Can I See?

As I was walking throughout the night
Soft, deep voices
Spine-chilling sprites wandering around
Zombies and witches hunting food
Wolves howling in the night sky
Trails of red, flaming red blood
Weak, old leaves falling from trees
Haunted houses
Full black sky
Fruit bats greedily sucking juice from apples
Vampires wandering off
In a blink of an eye
I wake up
Everything is perfectly fine.

Sara Howlader (9)
Gearies Primary School, Gants Hill

Dreams

D reams are a delightful start
R emember, they stay in your heart
E ach day the sun shoots light
A t night, you'll sleep with delight
M orning, night they're both beautiful
S o dreams are wonderful

L isten to your heart
O utstanding moments don't go fast
V arious times, various dreams
E very day, I just think about dreams!

Punyatoa Roy (9)
Gearies Primary School, Gants Hill

Rhymecraft

R hyming about Minecraft
H aving to make a ginormous house
Y odelling at the top of the house
M aking a garden
E normous cities
C reating an amazing city
R oaring with ideas
A ble to make it mind-blowing
F ighting for land
T ired after a busy day

This is how I play Minecraft.

Vinuki Vidara Buddhadasa (11)
Gearies Primary School, Gants Hill

Winter Wonderland

Magical land of shimmering snow,
When clumps of snowdrops start falling,
Glistening icicles start foaming.
Some animals start to hibernate,
Kids start touching the sparkly snowflakes.

Kids love the glittery snow,
It twinkles in the sun.
They start making snowmen,
Snowflakes on the land.
Kids love Winter Wonderland forever!

Manishaa Senthilkumaran (9)
Gearies Primary School, Gants Hill

Nightmare

N ever again shall I have this dream
I n my next dream, I want a laser beam
G ood things did not happen in my mind
H ope it does not happen next time
T onight in my mind, there shall be no clowns
M aybe I will not drown
A rgh!
R eally scary
E very night I shall remember this nightmare.

Rayaan Ahmed (9)
Gearies Primary School, Gants Hill

Gymnastics

G reat flexibility
Y ears and years of practice
M uch hard work and dedication
N ever giving up
A lways trying new skills
S plits, layouts and handsprings
T rying always to achieve a ten
I nspiring the new generation of gymnasts
C hampionship wins
S uccess is key.

Avneet Kaur Degun (10)
Gearies Primary School, Gants Hill

Happiness

H appiness is key
A little friendship won't be bad
P eople like to play
P ardon me, children like to play
I f someone is rude, don't play with them
N ever be rude to anyone else
E veryone is equal
S o remember your manners
S ome would say goodbye.

Forhad Al Mahfuz (10)
Gearies Primary School, Gants Hill

Autumn

I wonder what the autumn will bring,
Many colourful leaves that like to sing,
Leaves are hustling and munching,
Red, orange, brown leaves crunching,
The wind begins to blow,
The leaves are scattering fast and slow,
Leaves are falling to the ground,
Making a circle, big and round.

Faiza Shahid (9)
Gearies Primary School, Gants Hill

Blobats

When you mix a blob,
and you mix a bat,
squash them together,
and make a blobat!

Blobats eat beds and berries,
and other things,
that may be hairy.

Blobats sleep on people's heads,
while the people,
sleep in their beds.

Sriansh Panda (7)
Gearies Primary School, Gants Hill

How To Fight

Craft weapons and put in a slot,
You hurry up a lot,
It is night,
Keep a close sight,
Enemies might appear!
Attack them with a fear,
Build houses with a light
Or die with a creeper in your sight
Have a nice fight!

Bishal Roy (11)
Gearies Primary School, Gants Hill

I Am Seasons

It's cold and snowy,
I am winter.

I make flowers,
I am a photographer's dream,
I am spring.

It's hot,
I make people sweat,
I am summer.

I make leaves fall down,
I am autumn.

Parija Miral Popat (8)
Gearies Primary School, Gants Hill

Aliens Love Tea

A liens are angry, just like me
L et them drink lots of tea
I f they scream, give them more
E very day let us meet for tea
N ow that's a plan for sure!

Aksharra Vidhyaprakash
Gearies Primary School, Gants Hill

My Dream

Last night I had a dream
There was a mountain of ice cream!
It had plenty of colours

The queue was as long as a snake
I saw the ice cream become a waterfall!

Armaan Gorthy (8)
Gearies Primary School, Gants Hill

Mr Welly McTelly

Mr Welly McTelly is lazy,
He is also very crazy,
He eats chocolate all day,
In his own boring way,
He eats beans for dinner,
He always wants to be a winner.

Sufyan Akbar Rashid (10)
Gearies Primary School, Gants Hill

Rock Star Catastrophe

Once there was a boy named Jim
He went to a rock star who was ever so thin
They performed on a stage
With a lion in a cage
Then they fell into the bin.

Rok Gustav Folkson (7)
Gearies Primary School, Gants Hill

Family

My family, you see
They are precious
They're also kind to me
They are always in my heart
No matter what we do
We will never be apart.

Adyan Alam (7)
Gearies Primary School, Gants Hill

Crazy Dreams

I once had a dream
That was very weird
It was full of pumpkins
And I had a purple beard.

I once had a dream
My mum was a grasshopper
My dad was Kanye West
And my best friend was addicted to chicken breasts.

I once had a dream
Where people were orange goats
Cars were flies
And clouds were boats.

I once had a dream
I had some egg for breakfast
When I turned around
I was in Texas.

Sydney Maffey (10), Macie Lily Crosby & Sam
Gidea Park Primary School, Gidea Park

The Steampunk Airship

Steampunk airship, you may ask
What the hell is this?
Well, it's a science fiction machine with a steam-powered twist
My Minecraft creation is not to be missed
And yes, that's right, you've guessed it, it's a steampunk airship!

With a grey stone floor, lots of cogs and glass all around
Where you can sit and have peaceful thoughts without a single sound
It's floatation is so relaxing far above the ground
Minecraft's best airship, I hope it will be crowned!

It will take you anywhere you want based on your mood
Whether happy, sad or just in need of food
It's a way to travel in style, miles better than the Tube
So I'm sure after one go on my airship you'll be wooed!

Steampunk airship, now you know exactly what I've made
You can come and have a go but I expect to be paid!
I promise it will be the journey of a lifetime, don't be afraid
Steampunk Airship, luxury travel, all human-made!

Teddy Short (9)
Gidea Park Primary School, Gidea Park

Really?

'What d'you want for Christmas, dear?'
She said that year
'Well,' I said, 'there is one thing
I would really like...'
'Yes?' Mum replied

'Please can I have a dog?'
'No!
Too much hassle
Too much fuss
You've got carried away dreaming dear
A dog's just not for us.'

'What d'you want for Christmas, dear?'
She asked the next year
'How about a cat?'
'No!
Too scratchy
Have to buy too much tat
I don't want it coming in with a half-eaten rat!'

'What d'you want for Christmas, dear?'
She said for the third year
'But nothing
Furry
Scaly
Feathery
Slimy
Wet
Or alive!'

'Erm,' I replied
'I'll just have a book.'
'Really?
Can't you think of anything more interesting?'

Alexandra Hopkins (10)
Gidea Park Primary School, Gidea Park

Party Fun Poem

If you go to a party, you want to have some fun
There are balloons that you can play with so go and have some fun.
Pass the parcel you can play
I really think you should do so, definitely stay
It's present time, open them up, come on, I wonder what you've got?
Who wants to paint? Oh no, someone spilt a pot
Musical statues, you dance until your socks get blown off
Cake, come on everybody, have a bit of it
Wait, we forgot cards! Come on everybody, open one up
Show time, come on, let's see what you can do here
Water fight, *splish*, *splash*, everybody is soaked
Let's get everybody!
Yummy strawberries
Find the twigs, everybody found one, yeah let's play
No, please don't leave, stay!

Wink murder, people dying, uh-oh, quick!
Find the murderer
Come on everybody let's have some party fun

Eliza Dundas (7)
Great Totham Primary School, Great Totham

Minecraft Life

Minecraft life is full of adventure,
A world with no limits,
creating and building.

Searching for diamonds and emeralds,
to help fight against the mobs
and the enemy, Herobrine.

There are three dimension to play in.
Beware of the red and orange lava
in the Nether dimension

It's peaceful and fun,
Playing in the Overworld
but at night we scream and run.

The end is in sight,
When we reach the end dimension
fighting the boss to win and survive.

Toby Woodman (7)
Great Totham Primary School, Great Totham

Raindrops And Flowers

Raindrops falling from the sky
Pitter-patter, pitter-patter
From the dark grey clouds way up high
Falling down to the squelchy, wet ground
Pitter-patter, pitter-patter
Listen to that sound.

Soon the rain stops and out comes the sun
Glowing, shining, sparkling bright
Look at the pretty flowers, here they come

Watch out flowers, here come the slugs and snails
Slimy, squelchy, sticky, gooey
Leaving trails from their tails.

Summer Nicole Jarvis (7)
Great Totham Primary School, Great Totham

Summer

I can feel the cold, swishing air on my feet
The ladybirds are tickling my tickly small feet
My tummy tickles in the air
The summer breeze is swishing around everyone
All of the snow and the leaves are blowing away
I can smell beautiful flowers
The pretty colours are coming back here
My hair is swishing in the air
It smells like rose petals
I can see some busy bees
They're chasing me
Argh!
Phew! The bees have gone home!

Lauren Ferguson (7)
Great Totham Primary School, Great Totham

Monkeys

Monkeys swing through trees, they eat bananas and laugh, 'He he he!'
Monkeys have dangling long tails and hang upside down on a branch
Monkeys live in the jungle, a dangerous place
They will jump out and say, 'Boo! He he he!'
Monkeys pick flies out of other monkeys
Then they eat them, yuck!
People once were monkeys
What a surprise!
Can you imagine us those cheeky things?

Emily Seabright (7)
Great Totham Primary School, Great Totham

Flowers In Spring

Flowers in the sun, look so pretty
Flowers in the dark, look so dark
Flowers in spring make me want to sing
Flowers in the spring
So tall and bright, what a beautiful sight
Petals make the flower look so colourful
Flowers in the spring are so tall and colourful
Flowers are so tall, they look like a tower
Flowers are so powerful.

Gracie-Lou Redgrove (7)
Great Totham Primary School, Great Totham

In The Sky

Like a bird soaring down
The plane started dropping
It thrived, but dived
The engine spitting and popping.

Like a ball in the sky
The bird was black and blue
It swiftly flew up and down
It did a sneeze, 'Atchoo!'

Like candyfloss
The cloud was bulgy
It moved like a snail
So pale, so pale.

Emma Hull (7)
Great Totham Primary School, Great Totham

Butterflies

B eautiful butterflies
U nique in every way
T hey are as delicate as a leaf
T here are lots of different types
E very colour of the rainbow
R ed Admirals, Adonis Blue, Painted Lady
F laps its wings gently
L ikes to collect pollen from plants
Y ellow, red and blue colours.

Jake Sutton Moss (7)
Great Totham Primary School, Great Totham

The Boy Who Wanted To Dance

There once was a boy from France
Who moved to London to dance
He stepped to the right, he jumped to the left
But all he could do was prance
He turned around, hit the ground
And ended up in a trance
In his trance, he dreamed to dance
In the end he went back to France!

Haydn Court (7)
Great Totham Primary School, Great Totham

All The Fruits

Fruit is very tasty to eat
I like to eat it as a treat
Apples, grapes, bananas, pears
Grow strong bones, body and hair
They come in all sizes and shapes
Long bananas and round juicy grapes
If I want to be strong and play
I need to eat my five-a-day!

Molly Anna Surgett (7)
Great Totham Primary School, Great Totham

On The Playground

On the playground we all play
Like any ordinary other day
Football, gymnastics we all do
But sometimes we all need the loo

We get hurt and scrape our knees
Sometimes we get stung by bees
We may get bullied or not
But we get back together again.

Rose Poppy Surgett (7)
Great Totham Primary School, Great Totham

Spring Days

I love spring

Such as the things it brings
Bees are buzzing as buzzy as can be
The birds singing their songs to me
The flowers are colourful and fresh to breathe
I love the smell that spring brings to me.

I love spring.

Autumn-Rose Heeley (7)
Great Totham Primary School, Great Totham

A Monkey Called Timmy

There once was a young monkey called Timmy.
He had a best friend called Jimmy.
They swung through the trees
And played in the breeze
Until they felt a bit spinny.

Lucy White (7)
Great Totham Primary School, Great Totham

Shocked

Shake, shake, the pen drops onto the wooden floor
Someone slams the giant door
The startled scream went off, the woman startled the poor soldier
The nurse went to a folder
The scream dies down
She turns around
Finds him staring into space
She put the letter in front of his face
Showing him what he wrote
They heard another U-boat
He started to shake, out of control
She doubted that he would be able to stay at the hospital.

Summer Lambert (11)
Harwich Community Primary School & Nursery, Harwich

WWI

Come! Come! Quick! Quick!
A sound of a cry
But their feet weren't even dry

If, in some rushing dreams, you too could pace
Watch the red blood running down their face
With no proper food to eat
Their boots are filled with disgusting water

There are fat rats
That hide under the soldiers' hats
Their hanging faces, like a devil's, sick of sin
Behind the curtain, that we find them in.

Gracie White (10)
Harwich Community Primary School & Nursery, Harwich

WWI Life

Every time I walk in trenches, I wish there were benches
Every day I see the rats, thank god they aren't bats
Why do soldiers shoot their guns, the bullet count is tons
All day and all night, digging trenches is a fright
Women at home in the kitchens, while we're digging the ditches
None of us go in no-man's-land, because that place is banned
We dream about dead, then we realise we're in bed.

Drew Beezley (10)
Harwich Community Primary School & Nursery, Harwich

Best Friend

Katie is my best friend
Our friendship will never end
She is very kind
And she will never leave me behind

We are always together
Best friends forever
I'm her only best friend
Because I'm round the bend

Our friendship is protected by a net
And she will never have another best friend
I bet!
Our friendship is in the sky
While we never say goodbye.

Chelsea Kelly (9)
Harwich Community Primary School & Nursery, Harwich

Trenches

T he dead bodies lay still
R ude soldiers celebrate after every kill
E verybody has their rifle and their knife
N ew soldiers are fearing for their life
C rying soldiers lie in the brown, wet mud
H olding their knife they fear, as it is covered in blood
E veryone is trying their best
S ometimes it's not easy when they are put to the test.

Maxim Bowgen (10)
Harwich Community Primary School & Nursery, Harwich

Sunny Days!

Whoosh! Whoosh!

The water was dancing, bobbing up and down
Then the circus came to town
Playing in the sun
Having so much fun
When you look down, you can see a puddle of ice cream
When you put suncream on your skin, you can see it gleam
The sand is scorching
You can hear people talking
Watch the sun going down
Hear the sea going back and forth.

Gracie Mae Kadar (9)
Harwich Community Primary School & Nursery, Harwich

Nurses

I am a nurse looking after soldiers
It's not nice seeing people die
Sometimes it makes me cry
I want to cry a mountain of tears
Sometimes soldiers even lose their ears!
Do you think you would cry
Seeing people of your team die?
I really don't like being a nurse
Sometimes I get cursed!
I go to the trenches every day
If someone is injured, I'm on my way!

Evangeline J Shephard (10)
Harwich Community Primary School & Nursery, Harwich

The Story Of A Nurse

I looked out the window
I saw men in the trench
I started to worry
I got a funny head
I went back to confused
I cried a flood of tears
I had no one left
I was not safe
I was in the middle of the war
I had to leave
I tried once, it didn't work
I tried again
I started to run
Not safe
I got killed for trying to be safe.

Caitlin Ruby Isabel Barham (10)
Harwich Community Primary School & Nursery, Harwich

My Friend Lola

She sings like a star
She is doing well so far
Such a good friend
It's her things that she lends

We are so alike
We both can't ride a bike
She is very funny
For a joke, she talks like a dummy

She has a few friends, guess who they are?
Anoushka, Ruby Coe, me and Kizz.

Sophie Louise Fuller (9)
Harwich Community Primary School & Nursery, Harwich

Dreams

D o you ever have a dream, a weird dream?
R ubbish dreams like you had to watch a kids' film
E lectricity went through your body and you woke up in hospital
A rabbit jumped on top of your head
M ickey Mouse gave you a big chocolate coin
S leep peacefully, my friend.

Henry Alexander Michael Lammas (9)
Harwich Community Primary School & Nursery, Harwich

Nurse Life!

I am a nurse from WWI
I experience a lot of deaths and blood, it's scary
Every day I get soldiers wounded, ill or shot nearly dead
I get floods of blood
I'm always so busy
Caves of soldiers and mountains of injuries
It is sad watching people die
I try my best
I am a nurse from WWI.

Eliza Betty Hyams-Morgan (10)
Harwich Community Primary School & Nursery, Harwich

Illness Is The Worst!

Shaking to death
Near enough on the last breath
Crawling on the bed
Just to rest my head
Getting a bit confused
It was keeping me quite amused
I didn't know what was happening
Nights were getting loud
Bang!
My life was what was happening

It was horrible!

Lily Knight (10)
Harwich Community Primary School & Nursery, Harwich

The First War

World War One was in trenches
There were no benches
You left your wife
You might lose your life
The rats grow as big as boulders
You could get trench foot from all the mud
Some of the bombs could be duds
It was horrible in the trenches
There were nasty stenches.

Kaceyleigh Garlick (10)
Harwich Community Primary School & Nursery, Harwich

Mai's Pig

M ud, mud, *splash splash*
A hairy pig and a super lovely girl
I love this friendship
S pecial friends forever

P ig and a friend
I hate it when they argue
G ood friends.

Penny Stacey (8)
Harwich Community Primary School & Nursery, Harwich

Riding In The Race

R iding out can be fun
I t can bring lots of opportunities your way
D own hill, up hill, around hills
I t can get you almost everywhere
N ow listen up, it is not luck to win a race
G o, go, go! That's how some do it

I t is all about communication with your horse
N othing can compare

T he thrill as the canter begins to start
H eart pounding as you gallop along
E dging towards the rider in front

R ough terrain unsettles some
A long the route, you go faster and faster
C areering but still in control
E xcitement as you reach your goal.

Olivia Stone (11)
Highfields Primary School, Lawford

My Cats

Jess is starving and miaowing for food
Tommy must be out, in a bad mood

He will be hunting, battling toads and snakes
She is at home with her foot on the brakes

Any loud noise will send Jess scurrying
But to a friendly neighbour with an open door, she'll be hurrying

Tommy, he has seen it all before
Never tempted by an open door

Now Jess I am cuddling as I'm falling asleep
As for Tommy, until the morning it will have to keep.

Isabelle Marshall (9)
Highfields Primary School, Lawford

Minecraft!

M inecraft! Minecraft! Minecraft!
I s a huge craft
N ow a huge Minecraft laugh
E ver seen Herobrine in your backyard?
C hristmas treats, chests to open and see
R unning from a zombie, don't get in his way and become his prey
A fter a long day, you lie down in your block-built house
F un, laugh, run and jump
T omorrow is going to be an even better play.

Molly Quinn Finch (9)
Highfields Primary School, Lawford

Digging In The Dark - A Rhyming Poem

Digging in the dark
Mining in the park
Saying hello dark
Doing your part.

Making a sword
Might sound bored
Running for your life
Having a knife.

Having a mod
Not having a dog
Looking in a cave
Better be brave!

Oh no, there's a creeper!
Better be a reaper!
I am not digging in the dark.

Joshua James Gerrard Bird (9)
Highfields Primary School, Lawford

The Ogre From Ogre Wood

The ogre from Ogre Wood has no name
For that, he has no fame
He is also fat and uses a bat

Ogre! Ogre!
Run away!
Build a villa
And don't be its
Prey!

Nicolas Kumai-Girard (9)
Highfields Primary School, Lawford

Lava And Magma

Lava and magma all the same
But those are powerful and insane
It is boiling hot
Really, really hot
But some people think it's right on the spot
Some people call it lava
Some people call it magma
Lava and magma have the same meaning
But it's just not the feeling
If you touch it you'll burn
But it also tells you to learn
You can use it for cooking
Only when someone's not looking
When a volcano erupts
It does a cluck
All the lava and magma coming out
The eruption making the atmosphere so loud.

Rhemson Nzolameso (9)
Parsloes Primary School, Dagenham

Minecraft Journey!

When I explore
I find a door
Oh no, Herobrine!
I found a sign
When I mine
I always sigh
The disgusting dirt
I am such a button
But who wants mutton?
The Enderman's eyes gleam like the moon in the sky
It makes me want to fly
I love diamonds, they're as shiny as gold.

Zbigniew Chertlur (8)
Parsloes Primary School, Dagenham

Practical Pirates

P ractical, powerful and peckish pirates
I nterfering, intelligent and inflexible pirates
R esponsible, repulsive and repellant pirates
A rgentinian, abandoned and arrogant pirates
T hreatening, terrifying and tiring pirates
E vil, exhausting and electrifying pirates
S neaky, sly and scuttling pirates.

Joseph Archer (7)
Priory Primary School, Bicknacre

Peckish Pirates

P eckish, picky and playful pirates
I maginative, impatient and interesting pirates
R idiculous, reckless and ripping pirates
A dventurous, average and awful pirates
T raditional, terrific and terrifying pirates
E nthusiastic, exhausting and elegant pirates
S limy, sliding and scuttling pirates.

Esther Stickley (8)
Priory Primary School, Bicknacre

Popular Pirates

P opular, powerful and prying pirates
I ncisive, independent and impressive pirates
R ich, relaxing and ready pirates
A musing, alarming and annoying pirates
T errific, threatening and thoughtless pirates
E nergetic, eager and enthusiastic pirates
S neaky, sly and sword-slashing pirates.

Isabella Crome (8)
Priory Primary School, Bicknacre

Polished Pirates

P olished, peevish and panicked pirates
I nteresting, incensed and investive pirates
R uthless, reserved and ruffled pirates
A shamed, artistic and agile pirates
T rusting, terrific and terrifying pirates
E ntertained, extraordinary and envious pirates
S ly, swift and shouting pirates.

Eleanor Border (8)
Priory Primary School, Bicknacre

Pin-Dropping Pirates

P in-dropping, pesky and prickly pirates
I ncandescent, indecisive and inky pirates
R estful, resourceful and restless pirates
A dventurous, affable and agile pirates
T ight-lipped, tiring and tough pirates
E xtrovert, enthralling and exciting pirates
S ly, secure and sticky pirates.

Alana Lloyd (8)
Priory Primary School, Bicknacre

Paunchy Pirates

P aunchy, peeved and pesky pirates
I nflexible, intent and intelligent pirates
R epellant, ripping and rich pirates
A shamed, astonished and attractive pirates
T ense, terrifying and tender pirates
E mbarrassed, edgy and empowered pirates
S muggling, spying and scallywag pirates.

Darcy Sofia Rogers (7)
Priory Primary School, Bicknacre

Peaceful Pirates

P eaceful, pure and picky pirates
I ndignant, independent and inexperienced pirates
R idiculous, rich and ready pirates
A dventurous, awesome and angry pirates
T ouchy, thrilling and threatening pirates
E motional, eager and easy pirates
S neaky, swashbuckling and super pirates.

Ruby-Tallulah Smith (8)
Priory Primary School, Bicknacre

Picky Pirates

P icky, poised and purposeful pirates
I mpressive, impure and impressing pirates
R esponsible, rich and reckless pirates
A merican, awkward and adventurous pirates
T eenaged, troubling and threatening pirates
E vil, exhausted and eager pirates
S ly, smuggling and secret pirates.

Ellie-Rae Ward (7)
Priory Primary School, Bicknacre

Powerful Pirates

P owerful, pesky and perky pirates
I ndolent, important and incisive pirates
R epellant, red and rattling pirates
A merican, ancient and angry pirates
T hrilling, traditional and teenage pirates
E vil, eager and electric pirates
S ecret, spying and swashbuckling pirates.

Jude Platt (7)
Priory Primary School, Bicknacre

Powerful Pirates

P owerful, poor and positive pirates
I nventive, important and involved pirates
R adical, realistic and relaxed pirates
A fraid, able and agleam pirates
T errible, twinkly and terrifying pirates
E lectric, evil and easy pirates
S uper, skinny and speedy pirates.

Marina Burchea (7)
Priory Primary School, Bicknacre

Polish Putrid

P esky, putrid and powerful pirates
I ntent, illogical and impossible pirates
R osy, ripping and ruthless pirates
A pparitional, arch and ardent pirates
T empting, tanned and thriving pirates
E ternal, endearing and embarrassed pirates
S neaky, sly and swashbuckling pirates.

Alfie Webb (7)
Priory Primary School, Bicknacre

Sneaky Scallywags

P oor, pesky and powerful pirates
I mpolite, impatient and impure pirates
R eckless, ready and realistic pirates
A ngry, anxious and animated pirates
T hin, tiny and terrific pirates
E ager, embarrassed and entertaining pirates
S trange, sneaky and strong pirates.

Jamie Russell (7)
Priory Primary School, Bicknacre

Poison Pirates

P oison, porky and picky pirates
I mpure, illogical and independent pirates
R uthless, rich and reckless pirates
A merican, awkward and awesome pirates
T rustful, thin and thrilled pirates
E xhausted, empty and eager pirates
S washbuckling, scary and shouting pirates.

Callum Lowe (7)
Priory Primary School, Bicknacre

Polish Pirates

P olish, putrid and powerful pirates
I ntent, illogical and impolite pirates
R ipping, raw and ruthless pirates
A ngry, Argentinian and athletic pirates
T errific, thwarted and tidy pirates
E ternal, endearing and embarrassed pirates
S pying, silent and scary pirates.

Drew Almond (7)
Priory Primary School, Bicknacre

Pasty Pirates

P asty, powerful and picky pirates
I ntent, inflexible and illogical pirates
R ude, raw and rich pirates
A merican, angry and amusing pirates
T roubled, tricky and threatening pirates
E lectronic, entertaining, edgy pirates
S washbuckling, stealing and sneaky pirates.

Molly Rosam (8)
Priory Primary School, Bicknacre

Painted Pirates

P ainted, pesky and picky pirates
I tchy, irritable and intolerant pirates
R eliable, reposeful and remorseful pirates
A vid, awful and awesome pirates
T hick, twinkly and terrific pirates
E ndearing, enticing and electrifying pirates
S pying, sliding and slippery pirates.

Beth Miller (7)
Priory Primary School, Bicknacre

Pure Pirates

P ure, pleased and plucky pirates
I mpossible, impressive and imaginative pirates
R uthless, rosy and raw pirates
A dvanced, angry and alarmed pirates
T all, terrifying and empty pirates
E vil, energetic and empty pirates
S ly, silent and scary pirates.

Jessica Meadow Healey (7)
Priory Primary School, Bicknacre

Plundering Pirates

P lundering, peckish and plucky pirates
I ndecisive, independent and indigo pirates
R ich, restless and rude pirates
A thletic, avid and alert pirates
T all, tearful and thin pirates
E vil, eager and elderly pirates
S neaky, savage and stinking pirates.

Thomas Power (8)
Priory Primary School, Bicknacre

Pure Pirates

P ure, popular and pinchy pirates
I mpure, impolite and impulsive pirates
R elaxing, rumpled and rumbly pirates
A ngry, American and awful pirates
T ired, trustful and teenage pirates
E ager, edgy and eerie pirates
S ecret, silent and scavenging pirates.

Luca Chatten (8)
Priory Primary School, Bicknacre

Picky Pirates

P icky, powerful and panicky pirates
I nflexible, itchy and inspired pirates
R ich, relaxed and rosy pirates
A wful, American and artless pirates
T all, talented and thrilled pirates
E vil, envious and endless pirates
S uper, speedy and scary pirates.

Lily Morrish (7)
Priory Primary School, Bicknacre

The Four Seasons

The first season is spring,
When daffodils appear,
Baby lambs are born,
It's a wonderful time of year.

The second season is summer,
When we enjoy jumping in the pool,
Many go on holiday,
And wear sunglasses that are cool.

The third season is autumn,
Conkers and acorns fall from the trees,
The nights become darker,
As we walk through lots of crispy, fallen leaves.

The last season is winter,
The Christmas lights twinkle and glow,
Leading up to Christmas,
We really wish and hope for snow.

Emma Beardwell (10)
St Anne Line Catholic Junior School, Wickhay

Monsters

M onsters hide under your bed
O uch! They can bite you on the head
N ever go close to a monster
S tay close to your teddy bear
T ightly cuddle him
E ven though it might be weird
R emember not to go close to a monster
S ecretly, while they're asleep, whack the monster hard and it'll stay asleep forever.

Joel Jibu (10)
St Anne Line Catholic Junior School, Wickhay

Unicorns And Rainbows

Unicorns and rainbows,
are brothers and sisters.

Unicorns and rainbows,
love each other.

Unicorns and rainbows,
are like you and me.

Unicorns and rainbows,
shall be free.

Unicorns and rainbows,
till the end.

Unicorns and rainbows,
are best friends.

Tyra Nyakunengwa (10)
St Anne Line Catholic Junior School, Wickhay

My Trusty Diamond Sword!

As I dig in the night,
In the cave,
I find treasure beyond my dreams,
Oh, what do I do? Oh what do I do?
Make a diamond sword or a diamond hoe?

I make a decision and make a diamond sword,
I go to the dungeon and kill all the mobs,
Oh what do I do next? Oh, what do I do next
With my beautiful diamond sword?

Steve Nevin (10)
St Anne Line Catholic Junior School, Wickhay

Pokémon Alola Region

Walking in the dark forest
Seeking the amazing Pokémon
Keep a close eye for what you are searching for
Tapu Bulu, Tapu Fini, Tapu Koko and Tapu Lele
They are hard to get
They also look for you!
Team Rocket! Team Rocket!
Watch out for them!
They might steal your Pokémon.

Gabriel Kijanczuk (9)
St Anne Line Catholic Junior School, Wickhay

Monster Under My Bed

M any monsters are cruel, many monsters are cool
O n dark nights they sneak under your bed and hide
N aughty monsters bite
S illy monsters fight
T iny monsters get under your feet
E nding up as squishy meat
R avenous monsters eat you up!

Tonna Obidi (10)
St Anne Line Catholic Junior School, Wickhay

Wait In Hope

W e all wait for the silence to clear
A pin drop in the room, we can all hear
I nervously wait, my heart pounding like a mouse
T o hear the results, good or maybe bad

I n the room, everyone's sitting like statues
N ight we still wait, then it will come to day again

H ope we say in our minds that it will be good news
O n the chairs, we are sitting, sweating like pigs
P atience, they say, it's a skill, but not for now, we are nervous
E verywhere, the world is still, the crack of dawn and nobody moves...

Michelle Mpamugo (10)
St Joseph's Catholic Primary School, Dagenham

Minecraft My Usual Doom!

In the deep, dark caves the diamonds gleam
Danger's all around, it seems
The creepers sneak and zombies call
While spiders are climbing up the wall
Your picks near out, your shovel too
There's still so much more that you can do!
So much coal and iron and gold to find
You wonder if you still have time
'Just one more block! One more!' you say
But an unseen hole is in your way
You slip, you fall in the lava you go!
And burn up to a crisp, all nice and slow...
With that, you're done, your stuff is gone
All that work, it took so long!
You found iron and gold and diamonds too
Then into the lava right out of the blue
You head back home with a crestfallen sigh
Unable to believe you let yourself die!
You quit the game right there and then
Knowing you'll eventually be back again
For now the lava's won the day

And taken all your stuff again!
Now sit back and relax in the safety and comfort of your room
Wait, what's that noise?
Ssss, boom!

Favour Omoradion (10)
St Joseph's Catholic Primary School, Dagenham

Beware Of The Creeper

Beware of the creeper,
So crumpled and green.
Hissing in the light,
Exploding at night.

Beware of the creeper,
So horrid and mean.
You can shoot it with an arrow, kill it with a sword
But you would just see more, then eventually get bored.

Beware of the creeper,
A killer at its worst,
It will make your screen go crimson-red,
And bear the words, 'You're dead...'

Beware of the creeper!

Stephaine Fope Akinnawonu (10)
St Joseph's Catholic Primary School, Dagenham

My Hobby: Art

As I do my amazing art,
There's a warm feeling in my heart.
Painting the wonderful trees,
Swaying in the breeze.
My white paper talks and says to me,
'Draw a beautiful bee.'

The canvas is as colourful as a rainbow,
People look and say, 'Whoa!'
I draw and draw and draw,
A luxurious lion's claw,
And never, ever stop!

For me, art is like a tree,
Pictures growing up and up...

Emile Zubkus (8)
St Joseph's Catholic Primary School, Dagenham

A Crazy Canary

A canary speaks
Along his shiny beak
Like a baby baboon
Though he does love a giant balloon
He is as dumb as a rock
And his mind is really blocked
Then he found something round
He banged it on the ground
While the tearful baby cries
He loves to dangerously dive
Though he is as mad as a clown
He has a shiny crown
Here lies the crazy canary.

Lexi Cooper (8)
St Joseph's Catholic Primary School, Dagenham

Majestic Kingdom

I was walking down on the street
I thought to myself about animals
Lions are fierce and strong, king of its own world
Giraffes as tall as a crane
To reach the highest building
Queen of its own world.

Cheetahs as fast as tornadoes to reach its bride
Butterflies as gentle as can be
Flying through the wonderful kingdom.

Tomiwa Alaitan (9)
St Joseph's Catholic Primary School, Dagenham

Art Wonders

P aint, gloopy in the palette
A mazing, shimmering colours
I t transforms into a rainbow
N o glum, dark colours
T he bright colours make joy
I n my grumpy days
N o sadness comes to my heart
G reen, orange and red wonders in my head.

Amelia Clare Lloyd (7)
St Joseph's Catholic Primary School, Dagenham

Baking A Cake

B aking a cake
A ching, full of hunger
K ale isn't good enough!
I think it's as bad as thunder
N icely chuck the flour in
G iving milk to spare

A dding in the eggs

C ake needs sugar, it's always there
A ll you need to do now is
K ick around and wait
E njoy! You have now got your cake!

Zack Cristescu (10)
Trinity School, Kelvedon Hatch

Seasons, Oh Wonderful Seasons

Autumn, winter, summer and spring,
All these seasons make me sing.
Winter comes with its cold, icy chills
With snowmen, presents and sugar-coated hills.
This makes winter such a thrill.

Spring's here and the bluebells have sprung.
Easter is on its way,
I can't wait for the Easter holiday.

Here comes summer with the burst of a hot flaming sun,
Warming our hearts with long hot days,
Making us thirst for a nice cold lemonade.

Autumn appears, covering the ground with golden leaves,
Suddenly! All the trees are bare,
Getting ready for the chilly snow, soon to come in the winter.

Autumn, winter, summer and spring
Oh, how I love what you bring.

Joy Mungai-Kimani (10)
Trinity School, Kelvedon Hatch

YOUNG WRITERS INFORMATION

We hope you have enjoyed reading this book – and that you will continue to in the coming years.

If you're a young writer who enjoys reading and creative writing, or the parent of an enthusiastic poet or story writer, do visit our website **www.youngwriters.co.uk**. Here you will find free competitions, workshops and games, as well as recommended reads, a poetry glossary and our blog.

If you would like to order further copies of this book, or any of our other titles, then please give us a call or visit **www.youngwriters.co.uk**.

Young Writers
Remus House
Coltsfoot Drive
Peterborough
PE2 9BF
(01733) 890066
info@youngwriters.co.uk